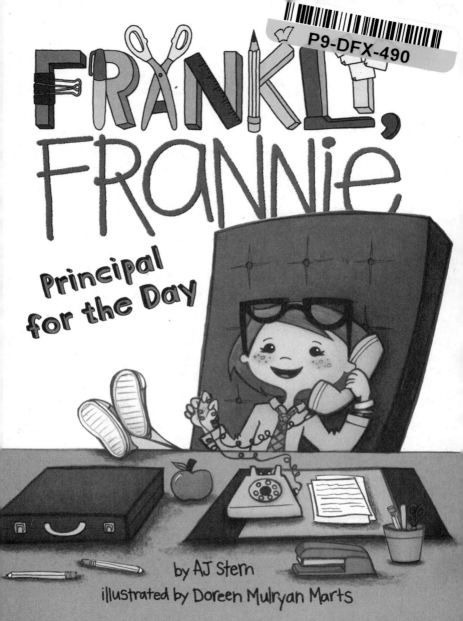

FRANKLY, FRANNIE

Principal for the Day

by AJ Stern

illustrated by Doreen Mulryan Marts

Grosset & Dunlap
An Imprint of Penguin Group (USA) Inc.

For Kara, of course.

Thanks as always to everyone at Penguin: Francesco
Sedita, Bonnie Bader, Caroline Sun, Scottie Bowditch,
and my editor, Jordan Hamessley, and also, of course, to
Doreen Mulryan Marts, who draws Frannie just like I'd
pictured her. Your support and enthusiasm is unparalleled!
To Julie Barer, who negotiates like nobody's business
and to my family and friends for their support. And of
course to my nieces and nephews: Maisie, Mia, Lili, Adam,
and Nathan, without whom I'd have lost touch long ago
with the bane and beauty of kid linguistics.—AJS

GROSSET & DUNLAP
Published by the Penguin Group
Penguin Group (USA) Inc., 375 Hudson Street, New York, New York 10014, USA
Penguin Group (Canada), 90 Eglinton Avenue East, Suite 700, Toronto,
Ontario M4P 2Y3, Canada (a division of Pearson Penguin Canada Inc.)
Penguin Books Ltd., 80 Strand, London WC2R 0RL, England
Penguin Group Ireland, 25 St. Stephen's Green, Dublin 2, Ireland
(a division of Penguin Books Ltd.)
Penguin Group (Australia), 250 Camberwell Road, Camberwell, Victoria 3124,
Australia (a division of Pearson Australia Group Pty. Ltd.)
Penguin Books India Pvt. Ltd., 11 Community Centre,
Panchsheel Park, New Delhi—110 017, India
Penguin Group (NZ), 67 Apollo Drive, Rosedale, Auckland 0632, New Zealand
(a division of Pearson New Zealand Ltd.)
Penguin Books (South Africa) (Pty.) Ltd., 24 Sturdee Avenue,
Rosebank, Johannesburg 2196, South Africa

Penguin Books Ltd., Registered Offices: 80 Strand, London WC2R 0RL, England

Text copyright © 2011 by AJ Stern. Illustrations copyright © 2011 by Penguin Group
(USA) Inc. All rights reserved. Published by Grosset & Dunlap, a division of Penguin
Young Readers Group, 345 Hudson Street, New York, New York 10014.
GROSSET & DUNLAP is a trademark of Penguin Group (USA) Inc. Printed in the U.S.A.

Library of Congress Control Number: 2010050520

ISBN 978-0-448-45542-6 (pbk)   10 9 8 7 6 5 4 3
ISBN 978-0-448-45543-3 (hc)   10 9 8 7 6 5 4 3 2 1

CHAPTER

On Monday at exactly **noon o'clock**, our teacher, Mrs. Pellington, took us to the auditorium. She said there was a special surprise coming, but when we got there, we only saw other kids. It is a scientific fact that seeing other kids at school is not a surprise.

Once we got settled, Principal Wilkins came out onstage, and that is when everyone got very **excitified**. This is because hearing special news is like opening a present. You know it is going to be very good, but you don't know what it is until all the paper is off.

"I know you're going to want to hear this announcement! This isn't something you want to miss," Principal Wilkins called out, waving his arms in the air. Then he went over to the microphone and spoke right into the silver ball of it.

"If I can have your attention, please!" he yelled. "I have some news you'll want to hear." And that is when everyone got quiet.

"In honor of American Education Week, Chester Elementary is starting a tradition. From now on, we will hold a contest every year to decide which lucky student will be Principal for the Day—"

When he said this, almost everyone flew out of their seats and through the ceiling. That is how **amazingish** we felt to hear this news.

Then he had to wave his hands again to get us to be quiet. "To enter the contest, each student must submit a composition that best explains why he or she wants to be Principal for the Day. The student with the best essay wins!"

One composition is not very much. I knew certainly that I could write at least **forty-five** compositions about jobs and why I wanted them. I could also write forty-five compositions about why Principal for the Day was the most **amazing** day my ears had ever heard of.

When I looked at my best friend

Elliott's face, I knew he agreed. He didn't even have to agree with his words or even a nod of his head. His eyes were so **wide-openish** I could see right into his brain thoughts, and his brain thoughts were, *Principal for the Day is the most amazing day my ears have ever heard of.* Elliott and I agree on almost everything. That is why we are best friends.

"Now," Principal Wilkins continued, "don't think this is an easy

job. You'll have to do actual work. There will be a list of tasks for you to follow. If you follow them well and complete your job to my satisfaction, there is another prize waiting for you."

When he said *another prize*, everyone got excited again.

"At the end of the winner's special day, he or she will give a presentation to the entire school about what it was like being Principal for the Day."

My ears were so excited that I thought they were going to **fall out of my head** and roll across the floor. I could already see myself up on the stage wearing my principal suit and carrying my principal briefcase.

"Your compositions are due on my desk by nine AM next Monday morning," Principal Wilkins told us. Even though that was one entire week away, I knew I could write my composition by tomorrow at 6:00 AM!

"When do we find out if we won?" someone in the very back yelled at the top of his yelling voice.

"After I've read all the compositions, I will come to the winner's classroom and make the announcement," Principal Wilkins continued. "Let's try and raise our hands when we have questions from now on, please."

I looked around the rest of the room, and that's when I realized how many compositions Principal Wilkins would have to read. There were probably **four hundrety** kids in this room. If I wanted to win, I had to work really hard on this composition. There is nothing in the world that I want more than an office. And an assistant. And the chance to hold my very own assembly. Onstage. At a podium. Talking into the silver ball of a microphone.

CHAPTER

"I'm home!" I yelled to my mother as I ran straight into my office, which is actually a desk in my bedroom.

"Hi, home!" my mom yelled, teasing me because I said I was home, when really I am Frannie!

I pulled out my **sharpest** pencil and my most professional-looking paper. The kind that did not have any holes on the side. Then I set out to write the best composition of **foreverteen**.

I stared at the blank paper and when no words filled my brain screen, I decided my pencil could be **sharpier**. I sharpened it and then tried again. Still nothing came into my brain. *Why* did I want to be Principal for the Day? I am not a specialist in answering about *whys*. I am much better at answering *whats*, but this was not a *what* thing. It was a *why* thing, and I was **stumpified**.

Sometimes when my brain won't do what I need it to, I send it on a vacation. It's a scientific fact that when I need to think of something, my brain thinks better when I'm not using the thinking part. Which is a for instance of why I started hula-hooping. I did about **four bachillion roundy-rounds** when I got a **geniusal** idea for my composition! I ran over to my desk and started writing as fast as I could before all the words leaked out of me.

PRINCIPAL FOR
THE DAY COMPOSITION
by MRS. FRANKLY B. MILLER

I am a person who loves jobs and offices. I already have a résumé, which is a list of all the places I've worked. I even have business cards. I have never been a principal of a school, not even for a day. The reason that I want to be Principal for the Day is that I am a really helpful kind of person. And I know principals are helpful, because Principal Wilkins has helped me with a lot of things. A for instance about this happened last year. I could not remember the order of the planets. Principal Wilkins said if I make a sentence with words beginning with the first letter of each word I need to remember, I will remember what I keep forgetting. And that is true because I still remember the order of the planets (Sun, Mercury, Venus, Earth, Mars, Jupiter, Saturn, Uranus, Neptune!) because of this sentence: **S**o **M**any **V**ery **E**arly **M**ornings **J**ust **S**miling **U**ntil **N**ight. I told everyone in my class about this trick, and when it came time to recite the order of the planets in front of our class, everyone remembered! All because of Principal Wilkins's good idea.

Another for instance about this job that I think is very important has to do with caring about other people. Even people you don't know! Every year Principal Wilkins has us bring in toys for children who don't get presents with their Christmases. Then we wrap them up really funly and send them to the kids. When they write us thank-you notes, the biggest ball of happiness fills my stomach.

I love that feeling so much. I would love to do something like this, but not this exact thing, because Principal Wilkins already does it. Maybe I would have everyone bring in a sweater for people who get cold but don't have warm things! Then, when I got their thank-you letters, I would get a warm ball feeling in my belly because I would know they were not cold anymore.

These are the things I would do as Principal for the Day. Even if I don't get this job, this is a for instance of something I would like to do, anyway.

After **thirteenish** years, I was finally done, and I ran downstairs to the kitchen to show my mom. She held it in her own hands and read it very carefully. When her eyes crinkled at the corners and she had **smile curls**, I knew it was a **geniusal** composition. I'm very smart about smile curls.

"Frannie, you have the biggest heart in America," my mom said. "This is an excellent composition. Whether or not you win, I think you should be very proud of yourself. I, for one, am VERY proud of you."

"Really?" I asked. I felt a lot of **pride-itity** that my mom thought that.

"Without question, this is the best composition you have ever written," she said.

"Dinner in ten minutes, okay?" she said, handing me back my contest composition. I nodded, too smiley to say anything, and then ran back to my room. I opened the top right drawer of my desk, which is where I keep all my office supplies, and pulled out my most

serious-looking pocket folder. I put
my contest composition in one inside
pocket. Then I opened the bottom right
desk drawer, which is where I keep all
my **jobbish** things, and pulled out my
résumé and a business card. I put those
in the other pocket. Then I went back to
the office supply drawer and pulled out
a large business envelope and slipped
the folder inside. The business envelope
is the exact color of mustard, which is
a very grown-up thing to like. Ketchup
is too **kiddish**. That is why they don't
make business envelopes in the color
of ketchup. After I sealed the envelope
shut, I got my **fanciest** silver pen and
wrote across the front:

MRS. FRANKLY B. MILLER,
FUTURE (?) PRINCIPAL
FOR THE DAY.

CHAPTER

That week was the slowest week I have ever lived in my whole life. It took **eighteen-fifty** days for next Monday to come.

When I got to school Monday morning, everyone in my class was very **run-aroundy**. Mrs. Pellington said we had to be very settled before she collected our Principal for the Day compositions. I settled very fast because I wanted her to collect my composition first. When you are the very first of anything, everyone knows how **seriousal** you are.

However and nevertheless, she did not collect my composition first, and that is why a **big disappointment puddle** formed at my feet. But then you will never believe your ears about what happened next! Mrs. Pellington asked for a **volunteer** to bring the compositions down to Principal Wilkins's office. Everyone's hands were in the air, and Mrs. P. chose my exact hand actually!

After putting my composition on top, I ran down the hall as fast as I could. I waved to Cora, Mr. Wilkins's assistant, as I passed her desk and walked into Mr. Wilkins's office. I could not even believe my eyes when I saw Mr. Wilkins sitting at his desk, already going through a pile of Principal for the Day compositions!

Did everyone wake up at **zero o'clock** in the morning so they could hand theirs in first? That's when I remembered about standing out. My dad says it's important to stand out in business. You don't want to be like everyone else or no one will remember

about you. That is why I decided to use my **English accent**. When you are British sounding, people take you very seriously, and right then I needed to be taken very seriously.

"Gewdd moneng to you, Principull Wilkunns. Puleeze accept my resoomay and compazisssion fawh the kahntest!"

Then I handed him my class's pile of compositions with my mustard-colored envelope right on top. He looked very **impresstified** with my accent.

"Irish?" he asked.

"English," I corrected.

"Ah! Okay. Good choice. Thank you very much, Frances."

"You are certainly and honestly welcome, Principal Wilkins."

The rest of the day went by so slowly I could feel my own body grow, which is not something you are supposed to feel apparently. *Apparently* is a grown-up word I use when I am talking about things I don't have scientific facts about.

I tried to pay attention in all my classes, but I could not stop thinking about if Principal Wilkins was reading my composition at that very **exact** minute. I could tell everyone else was wondering the same thing, too.

Elliott was jumping his knees up and down, which he does only when he's nervous. Millicent, who's always reading, was looking up from her book toward the classroom door every few minutes. And if you don't already know this about Millicent, there isn't much that can make her look up from a book. That is how much she loves to read, actually and as a matter of fact.

At lunch, Elliott, Elizabeth, Millicent, and I stood in line together for tacos. I am a person who likes **crunchy** foods, which is a for instance of why I love school tacos. They are the hard shell kind. When I crunch down on something and it makes that loud cracking noise, I feel very professional and adult, indeed.

"If I win, I am going to turn the cafeteria into a hair and beauty shop," Elizabeth told us. I did not prefer this idea because **no one** serves crunchy food in a hair shop!

"Where will we eat?" Elliott asked.

Elizabeth shrugged. "Somewhere else. That's not part of my job," she said, which was not a scientific fact. Plus and besides, Principal Wilkins was never going to let Elizabeth open a hair and beauty shop because that didn't have anything to do with school.

"I would get rid of all the classes, and we would learn just by spending the whole day, every day, in the library reading," Millicent said. This sounded really boring, but it also made my stomach **flop** over a little because I worried Principal Wilkins would give *her* the job.

"If I win," Elliott said, "I would give the job to Frannie and be her assistant." I looked at Elliott with the biggest surprise of life in my eyeballs.

"You would?" I asked.

"Of course," he said.

"Thank you, Elliott," I said, feeling very big with **happiness** about what he just said. "I would let you be the coprincipal with me."

"Really?" he asked.

"Indeed and nevertheless," I told him.

"Why would you do something like that?" Elizabeth wanted to know.

"Because Frannie really wants the

job, and I'm not as workerish as she is," he explained.

Millicent and Elizabeth nodded because they understood. Everyone knows how workerish I am. It's just one of those scientific facts about me.

That was when I filled up with a **secret, horrendimous** worry that Elizabeth or Millicent might win Principal for the Day. I would have been happy for them, I guess. But I did not prefer that to happen.

After lunch we had a spelling bee, and I waited for Principal Wilkins to announce the winner, but he didn't come! He didn't come during science or math or even during art! How many hours does it take to read **twenty-hundred** compositions? If I got to be Principal for the Day, I was going to be much faster at reading compositions than Principal Wilkins was. When the entire school day finished and Principal Wilkins *still* hadn't come to our classroom, I decided that I was also going to be a much faster winner picker than he was.

CHAPTER

You will not even believe your ears about what happened next. The next morning when I walked into my classroom, the first person I saw was Principal Wilkins! He was standing right next to Mrs. Pellington! Even though I felt very **run-aroundy**, I settled into my seat because I could not wait to hear about the winner. Everyone else did the same thing when they got to class. Elizabeth sat down so fast that she didn't even take her coat off!

"Hello, kids," Principal Wilkins said. His hair looked extra black and shiny, and his tie looked very straight and professional.

"I read a lot of compositions for the Principal for the Day contest. There were so many good ones to choose from. This was not an easy decision by any means."

Elizabeth was wearing her "I know I won this contest" smile.

"I looked for a lot of things. Enthusiasm was one of them . . ."

Elizabeth smiled even harder.

"Good ideas were another."

Elizabeth smiled so hard her face almost **fell off**.

That's when I imagined Elizabeth making her big speech at the assembly, high up onstage, talking to the entire school using the microphone.

"But, finally, I looked for someone who had well-thought-out, good reasons why they wanted this job," said Principal Wilkins. "And that person is—"

Elizabeth got ready to stand up, and I got ready to hold all my tears inside my eyeballs. "Frances B. Miller!"

I looked at Elizabeth, confused. Then I looked at Elliott, then at Principal Wilkins, who stood in front of us with a big grin.

"What do you think about that, Frannie?" he asked.

"I . . . I . . . I can't even believe my own ears about this," I told him.

"Why don't you come to the front of the room and read your composition out loud to everyone?"

I won the job *and* I won reading my composition to the entire classroom? This was the **best live dream** I had ever had. I stood up and walked to the front of the classroom and took my composition from Principal Wilkins. Then I read the entire thing out loud.

When I was done, everyone clapped really hard. Everyone except for Elizabeth.

"Okay, thank you, everyone, for your attention. You can get back to your lessons now," said Principal Wilkins. Then he came next to me and said, "Frannie, before you start your job, there will be some conditions. Mrs. Pellington will walk you to my office at the end of the day so we can have a serious conversation. Okay?"

I nodded, but suddenly I had a really **bad day feeling** on my skin. People only had serious conversations in the principal's office when they were in trouble. I did not know what in the **worldwide of America** I could have already done!

CHAPTER

I wanted to hold Mrs. Pellington's hand on the walk to Principal Wilkins's office because I did not know what was going to happen. But I did not because holding hands with adults is something I prefer doing only outside of school.

Mr. Wilkins's assistant, Cora, told us to have a seat. As Mrs. P. and I sat and waited, Cora got up and put a fresh stack of paper in the printer tray. She smiled at me and I smiled back. As principal, I would probably get to touch lots of stacks of paper. Stacks of paper are **extremely official**, and that is not an opinion.

A **millionteen** minutes later, Principal Wilkins opened his door and we went inside and sat down. "Frannie, I'd like to congratulate you once again," Principal Wilkins said straight into my eyeballs.

"Thank you very much for your congratulations," I told him, looking exactly back into his eyeballs.

"Do you know why I asked you here?"

"Perhaps actually, you wanted to hire me for an actual real-life job?" I asked with a little whisper in my voice.

Mrs. P. and Principal Wilkins both

laughed just a little bit.

"No. I'm sorry to disappoint you, but that's not the reason," said Principal Wilkins.

"Oh," I said as all my **excited breath** was sucked out of my body.

"Your composition was the best one for all the reasons I mentioned earlier. Normally, we'd have no hesitation giving the job to you—"

"But," Mrs. Pellington interrupted, "because you have a knack for getting too curious for your own good: *Cambridge Magazine*, *The Sandy Sanders Show* . . . ," Mrs. P. said, making a list of all the class trips we'd taken that didn't actually end up perfectly. "We decided there would be a few conditions to the job."

I looked at Principal Wilkins to

see if Mrs. P. was right about this sentence. Principal Wilkins nodded his head yes.

"We've seen you get yourself into hot water one too many times, but we didn't think it was fair to *not* give you this job because you deserve it. So,

we've come up with a three-strikes-
and-you're-out policy," he said.

"Like in baseball?" I asked.

"Exactly," he said.

"Can you give me a for instance of
a strike, please?" I asked in my most
seriousal voice.

"Absolutely. Like I explained in assembly, there will be a list of tasks for you to follow. If you get creative about your job as principal and do things that are not on the task list, you will get a strike. If this happens three times, you'll be out."

"You mean you'll fire me?" I asked.

"I'd prefer to look at it as ending your role as Principal for the Day early. So, do you understand the rules?"

I nodded yes. That was really **actually and certainly** true. I did understand the rules. I just did not love them.

"Do you think you can do all that?" Mrs. Pellington asked me.

"Yes, I can. And that is not an opinion," I told her.

"Good. Then welcome aboard, Frannie," she said.

Then Principal Wilkins stood up and shook my hand. I shook his hand back because that is what you are **supposed** to do when someone gives you their hand to shake. Then Mrs. Pellington and I thanked him for his time and walked back to our own office, which was our classroom actually.

CHAPTER

I was so excited to tell my parents about my new job, I could barely even breathe! They were very **impresstified** with me, especially when I told them that Cora would be my assistant.

Before bed that night, I told them, "Tomorrow I will not be regular old Frannie. I will look the same, but I will also be different. That is because I am going to be a principal."

"Will we have to call you Principal

Miller?" my dad wanted to know.

"Principal Frankly B. Miller is what I prefer," I told him. "Frankly is my professional name, and that is not an opinion."

"But until then you're Frannie, right?" my mom asked.

"Yes," I told her.

"Good. Because it is time for Frannie to go to bed," she told me.

I did not know how in the world of ever I was going to sleep. I looked at my clock to make sure that my alarm was set. The red light was still on, so that meant yes, it was set. I was planning on getting to my first and only day of my new job at **7:00** AM, but Principal Wilkins said that school didn't start until **8:30** AM. That is why I said I'd be there at **7:30** AM, and

I would wait. Principal Wilkins said that was not something he would prefer. And that is why I agreed to get there at **8:00** AM with the rest of the staff, when he said I should.

As Principal for the Day, I was going to dress **exactly** like Principal Wilkins. A for instance of what I mean is that I was going to wear a blue, collared shirt and my dad's most beautiful magenta tie. Those were the exact colors I had seen Principal Wilkins wearing the day before.

What I did not know about him was everything else. I couldn't just *look* like Principal Wilkins, I had to act like him, too. But I did not know some very important things about him, like, what did he eat for breakfast? What did he do in his office all day besides shuffling papers and yelling at kids? Did he have any friends? Where did he live exactly? These were all the types of thoughts swirling around my brain when I guess I fell asleep. Because when I opened my eyes, it was the next day!

At breakfast, when my mom passed me the cereal, I decided that principals didn't eat cereal. She asked what exactly they did eat for breakfast. And that is when I said I didn't know because no one remembered to tell me!

"I bet they eat eggs," my dad said as he pulled a carton of eggs out of the refrigerator.

"Yes, eggs!" I told him. Eggs sounded very **principalish**. Also, my dad wears a suit to work just like Principal Wilkins. And do you know what my dad eats

for breakfast? EGGS!

"Scrambled, over easy, boiled, sunny-side up, or fried?" he asked.

This was my first **very big decision** of the day.

"Sunny-side up!" Because that's the kind of day I wanted to have.

After I ate breakfast and got dressed, I packed my briefcase with things I might need, like my dad's empty glasses frames, business cards, résumés, paper clips, and blank paper.

Then I **clip-clopped** the buttons of the case closed and ran down to the car where my mom was waiting. We got to school at 7:55 AM exactly. I kissed her very fast because I had only five minutes, and also because I didn't think principals kissed their moms before going to school.

I am not a late kind of person, which is why I ran up the stairs to the second floor and ran down the hall and into the office where Cora sat.

"He'll be here any minute, Frannie," Cora told me.

I scrunched my face at this sentence. I did not prefer that Principal Wilkins was late on my first and only day of my new job.

"My name is Frankly, actually," I told her. That is when she looked up and showed me her eyeballs, which looked a little confused.

"It's my professional name," I explained. "I use it for all my jobs."

Cora nodded and smiled because she understood about professional names and jobs.

"Very good. Frankly, it is."

Then I sat down and waited and waited and waited. Finally, after **thirty-five years and forty-seventeen days**, Principal Wilkins arrived.

"Good morning, Principal Miller," Principal Wilkins said to me. That is when I bowed and said, "Good morning to you, too."

"You look very professional in your tie," he told me.

"Thank you very much for your compliment," I said. I was very **impresstified** with how **businessish** my voice sounded.

Principal Wilkins pulled out a key chain, which had a neighborhood of keys on it. I made a **brain note** to get a key chain and a worldwide nation of keys. He unlocked his door, and although I'd already been in his office, he said he'd give me a tour. This was something I really preferred. Principal Wilkins showed me where he sat to do his hardest thinking.

"And in here," he said, opening a drawer at his waist, "is where I keep my doodle pad. You are welcome to use it when you have tough decisions to make."

My ears could not even believe this sentence. I did not realize that doodling was something adults knew how to do.

After he finished giving me the tour, Cora came in and looked at me with big, smiling eyeballs.

"So what do you think?" she asked.

"I like it," I told her

Then they **rocket-shipped** the swivel chair taller for me, and I sat where Principal Wilkins sits every single day of his life.

"Do you remember the three-strikes-and-you're-out policy?" Principal Wilkins asked me.

"Yes," I told him, because I did actually. Even though I did not like it.

"It's a good policy to remember, especially since you might be going over school rules with any misbehaving students who are sent to the principal's office today."

I stood up because sometimes I do that when I **absolutely** cannot believe something.

"Is that really true?" I asked.

"It *is* true. That said, I will be supervising you, so you won't get carried away. Now, is everything clear?" he asked.

"Yes, Principal Wilkins," I said.

"Everything is very clear."

"Good. I just want to go over your list of tasks, and then we can both start our days," he said.

We sat down at the desk and looked down at my list of tasks. It was not even close to the type of tasks I had hoped I'd have. A for instance of what I mean is that I hoped the task list would read like this:

- Please go to the closet and pick out as many office supplies as you want and take them home.
- Test all the buttons on the telephone, as well as the staplers, three-hole punches, and electric pencil sharpeners to make sure they work.
- Please try the school intercom.
- Please come up with brand-new classes to replace the boring

ones we already have.

- The school lunch is disgusting. What would you like to eat every day? Make a list and give it to Cora.

But instead, the list of tasks I got went like this:

- Make morning announcements.
- Review attendance sheets and create one master list of all the absentees.
- Make twelve photocopies of the absentee list and distribute to all of the faculty.
- Observe one student teacher in action and make a list of three things you think they did well.
- Meet with student teacher at lunch to discuss your notes.

"If you need anything, Cora will be right here with you. All right,

Frannie?" Principal Wilkins asked.

"Frankly," I reminded him.

"Frankly. Have a great day!" he said.

"You, too, Principal Wilkins!"

"If you need me, Cora, I'll be in the teachers' lounge. Don't be afraid to use my cell phone," he told her, making his eye sockets **very hugeish** so Cora could see all the white around them. That's how people make their eyeballs look when they are being extremely serious.

"You got it, Mr. Wilkins," she said.

Cora was sitting in a chair directly opposite me at my desk. She didn't need to tell me why she did this. I already knew. She did it because now she was my assistant.

I could not wait to give Cora her first job, which would be something off my extremely important, but sort of **strictish** list. But before I could say anything, Cora got out of her chair and walked to my side of the desk.

"It's eight thirty. Time for the morning announcements," she said.

That is when my stomach filled up with moths and butterflies.

Cora opened a **top secret** drawer and pulled out a **top secret** microphone and put it right in front of my own face. I did not know that's where Mr. Wilkins's microphone lived! Then Cora handed me the announcements, all typed up on school stationery.

"Are you ready?" Cora asked.

"Yes, I am exactly ready," I told her as my nerves surfboarded all over my insides. "No! Wait! I am not ready!" I said. I forgot all about my eyeglass

frames, which I packed because they are a very **principalish** thing to wear. I opened my dad's briefcase and put the frames on my face. Then I looked up at Cora. "Now I am ready."

"Just read the words exactly as they appear," she said.

Then Cora pushed a button, and I heard the inside of the microphone **humming** at me. When she nodded, that is when I knew that it was time to talk. I looked down at the paper, but decided I would say a little something of my own first.

"Hello, Chester Elementary School. This is Frankly B. Miller, and I will be your principal today. I have never been a principal before, so I am very excited about this job—"

Cora crossed her arms and tapped

her foot a little bit at me. That is why I said, "And now I will read the morning announcements."

After I read the announcements, which were very boring and said things about today's lunch monitor and after-school sports, I took off my glasses and Cora put the microphone away. Then Patricia Weller, from third grade, ran into the office with a stack of **very important-looking** papers.

"Here you go," Patricia said as she handed Cora the papers.

I could barely keep my own breath in my body when Cora turned and handed *me* the stack of papers!!!

"These are the attendance sheets for the lower school," she said. "You need to look them over and write down all the absent children on a separate piece of paper. Then we will need to make twelve copies of that list and distribute it to all the teachers."

Copies! I love copies. Making copies meant using the copy machine, which is my exact favorite kind of machine.

"I'm going to run to the bathroom, Frankly, all right?" Cora asked.

I nodded yes because it was all right.

"Try and be finished with that list by the time I come back, okay?"

I nodded my head okay. When she left the room, I spun around in the swivel chair several times and felt very important indeed. I looked down at the class lists and counted the *not here* kids, which equaled only six! I wrote them all down on a separate sheet in less than one half of a second.

Now I had free time!

In that free time I decided to be a **really spectacular principal** and introduce myself to every single class, so they knew who was principal exactly for the day. While I was at it, I would ask them if they needed anything or had any questions whatsoever about the morning announcements, or anything in the entire world, actually, as a matter of fact.

CHAPTER

I walked down the lower school hall toward the first-graders. I could not wait to open their door and talk to them as their actual principal! It was the most **excitified** I'd felt since I made the morning announcements. I wasn't going to be show-offish about it, but I knew that the little kids would be very happy to meet the person behind the mouth that made the morning announcements. Even the teachers would look at me with WOW in their eyes. I could already feel it, and it hadn't even happened yet!

Here is a scientific fact about interrupting a class. You are not allowed to interrupt a class for any reason, unless it is an emergency, you are a teacher, or you are the principal. I was never any of those things, which was why I never interrupted classes. But today I was **the best** of those things. As Principal for the Day, it was my job to make sure anyone who needed help with anything got it. If someone needed to remember the order of the planets, now was their chance to learn such things from their principal!

I peered in through the door of Mr. Peters's kindergarten class. He was sitting on the desk reading to his students. They were listening very carefully. Some had their chins in their hands and others had their heads jutted out like excited turtles. They were extremely **concentratish**. Whenever Principal Wilkins had to tell our class something, he would just open the door and come in. That is because principals don't have to knock first. I turned the knob on the classroom door and walked right in. When everyone looked up at me, I felt the **most official and professional** I'd felt all day.

"Hello to everyone in Mr. Peters's class," I said.

"Hi," they called back.

"May I help you with something, Frannie?" Mr. Peters asked me.

"Today my name is Frankly," I

corrected him. "And today I am your principal."

"Yes, we know. We all heard your announcement. Do you need something? You've interrupted us in the middle of a story," Mr. Peters told me.

"Oh," I said, feeling a couple of **moths fly up in my belly**. Mr. Peters's face was giving me a bad day feeling on my skin.

"I . . . I . . . I . . ." That is when I realized I had not thought of anything to say to the class. I had to think of something quickly, otherwise I would feel so **humilified**. That is when I got a geniusal idea.

"It's much more fun to hear stories when you have snacks," I said. That is when the class agreed with me by saying how much they wanted snacks.

I was already being really helpful!

"Calm down, everyone," Mr. Peters told them.

"We want snacks!" someone yelled.

"Yeah! Things are more fun with snacks," someone else called.

I looked at them and, because I am actually extremely smart about snacks, asked, "What sort of snacks do you want?"

"Twizzlers!" someone yelled out.

"Gummy bears! Soda! Swedish Fish!" other kids called.

"Frannie, what are you doing? You should be in your office doing your job, not interrupting classes that are in progress," said Mr. Peters in a maddish voice.

"But I'm the principal today. I can do whatever I want."

"No, you may not," he said as he

stood up and walked toward the door. He opened the door and then stood beside it. This meant he was asking me to leave, which I did **not** prefer.

"Principal Wilkins does not come by and ask if we need snacks," said Mr. Peters.

"That is because we are very different types of principals," I told him. "I'm a snack kind of principal, and he's not."

"Frannie, please. You need to go back to your office now."

I looked back at the class and then at Mr. Peters. That's when I realized why he was being so **scoldish**.

"I will get you a snack, too!" I told him. "Do you love cookies?" I asked.

That's when a lot of the kids started to yell for cookies, and Mr. Peters's face turned extremely pink like a very amazing sunset.

"Frances Miller, please leave my classroom right now," he said.

I turned to all the kids and shrugged, letting them know I would not be getting them snacks however and nevertheless. Then I slunked away toward the next classroom, where I was certainly going to be welcomed.

But to my **horrible** surprise, when I walked into Mrs. Baxter's first-grade classroom, she was worse than Mr. Peters!

"Frannie, can I help you?" she asked when I walked in.

"I wondered if anyone wanted any snacks," I said. "Eating is good for learning."

"Yes! Yes! Snacks!" the kids yelled.

"Frances, please leave immediately. You know better than to barge into a classroom." She didn't even get up. She just pointed to the door, which I walked to quickly. Her voice was very strictish. When I shut the door behind me, I heard the class chanting together, "Snacks! Snack! Snacks!"

Then I heard some stomping, and when I looked back, Mrs. Baxter was pulling down the shade on her classroom door.

Couldn't they see I was just trying to be helpful? Certainly my very own class would be very happy to see me. Besides, I couldn't wait to show them what being Principal for the Day looked like on me. They were going to be really **impresstified**. Especially Elliott. And also Mrs. Pellington. She'd see me and think, *Oh, silly me, thinking Frannie's curious hands would get the better of her. Look at her being so adult and responsible making sure everyone is okay. She is a genius of the earth!*

My classroom was at the very end of the hall. As I got closer to it, my heart started to get very **thumpish**. Then, just when I reached my arm out to turn the doorknob, a voice behind me asked, "What are you doing?" It was Cora.

"Introducing myself to everyone!" I told her.

"Didn't I tell you to wait for me in

the office?" she asked.

"I did wait," I said. "I just waited . . . in this direction."

"Frannie, I have a lot to do today. I don't have time to be chasing you around. I really need you to follow the rules, okay?" Cora said without a smile anywhere on her.

"Okay," I said, looking at the ground and feeling **a little bit baddish**. Then she took my hand and we walked back to my office.

"Sit back down, Frannie. You have a long to do list, and you've only gotten two of them done," she said.

I scrunched my face at Cora in my brain where she couldn't see it.

"Frankly," I reminded her. Then I looked back down at the list and read the second thing I was supposed to do:

Make twelve photocopies of the absentee list and distribute to all of the faculty.

I was excited that I got to photocopy so many pieces of paper. But I had a bad day feeling on my skin because I didn't get to show my class what I looked like being **Principal for the Entire Worldwide Day of America**. Hopefully, that wasn't anything a little photocopying couldn't fix.

Just after Cora and I got back to the office, Principal Wilkins walked in.

"Frannie, what were you doing interrupting classes?" he asked.

"I wanted to make sure everyone had what they needed," I explained.

"Is that on your list of tasks?" he asked.

I shook my head no.

"Did Cora tell you to do that?"

I shook my head no.

m afraid, then, that this is your
rst strike, Frannie."

That is when my heart fell all the
way to my feet and melted into a big
disappointment puddle.

"It is?" I asked him to make sure.

"I'm sorry to say, it is. Now, please,
stick to your tasks and do exactly as
Cora tells you. I don't want to have to
come back up here today," he said.

"Sorry, Principal Wilkins. I will,"
I said, looking at his shoes. I was too
horrendified to look at his face.

After he left, I showed Cora the
list of names I'd gathered so she could
see I did my job. Then we walked to
a room with *two* copy machines, a
coffeemaker, and a table with two
staplers, one three-hole punch, seven
small boxes of paper clips, two in/out

trays, a hugeish ball made exactly of only rubber bands, a box of tape, and about **forty-billion** glue sticks!

Cora explained how to use the copy machine and said, "You need to be very careful about wasting paper. So make sure you line the paper up just so. The more times we make a copy mistake, the more paper we waste, and that's very bad for trees. Do you understand?"

I nodded my head yes to Cora because I did understand.

Then Cora noticed the coffeepot. "How is there no coffee already?" she asked. I knew this was the type of question that I was not supposed to answer.

"I'll be back in one minute, Frankly. Just hit COPY to get started."

Then Cora quickly raced out of the
room.

To make sure the machine was not
broken, I decided to do a test. I put
my cheek on the glass, then pressed
COPY. When a picture of my cheek shot
out onto the tray, I thought it looked
really **fantastical**. That is why I put
the other cheek down, too, and pressed
COPY again. I copied my chin, my
forehead, and both of my ears. That is
when I knew that I was making a book,
actually. And if I was making a book,
I'd probably need to use the three-hole
punch because my book would be too
thick for stapling.

As I walked over to the three-hole punch, I noticed the label maker. I certainly and actually needed to label my book, so everyone would know what my book was about and also who made it. But before I could even get to that part, Cora came back.

"How'd it go?" she asked.

"Great!" I said.

When she asked if I had made twelve copies, I realized that she wasn't talking about my book. She was talking about the third task on my list.

"Oh," I said. "I didn't do *that* job yet."

"What have you been doing?"

"This!" I said, holding up my book.

"Frannie, didn't I just explain to you about wasting paper?" I was **shocktified** that Cora would think copying my face was a waste of paper.

"You just had your first strike only minutes ago. How can you already be up to your second?"

I did not realize this was a second strike type of situation.

"Do I really have a second strike?" I asked her.

"I'm afraid so," she said, taking the attendance papers from me to copy herself. I felt very humilified and also shocktified. Did I really have only one strike left? I was going to have to be **extra strict** with my mouth words and my curious hands.

Once Cora made the twelve copies, we went from classroom to classroom handing them out. I waved to everyone, and they waved back. That made me feel really important, indeed.

When we got back to the office, the phones were ringing their necks off.

"Frankly, go get your task list from your office while I deal with the phones, please." Cora had a frustrated look on her face again.

I raced into my office to get the list. On the way there, I noticed something **shiny and red** out of my eye edge. I turned to look, and on the wall in the corner was the most beautiful box I'd ever seen.

I didn't know that microphones lived in drawers, and I did not know that beautiful red boxes lived on walls! It had a big handle in the middle and right above it read PULL FOR FIRE. That is when I realized what it meant exactly. What it meant exactly was this is what Principal Wilkins pulled when he fired a teacher.

I wondered what happened when you pulled it. Did a little flag come up that said SORRY! YOU'RE FIRED! Did the person getting fired pull it or did the person doing the firing pull it? I was extremely and actually very curious to know what happened when you pulled that handle.

I stared at the box one more time before I went back to my desk. I had to hurry because I didn't want Cora to see I was not being **concentratish** on my task.

I quickly grabbed the task list off my desk and, just as I reached Cora's desk, Principal Wilkins came in.

"Frankly, are you ready to observe the student teachers?" he asked me. The student teachers were not students, actually. They were adults practicing to be teachers.

I nodded yes. I did not know I'd be going with Principal Wilkins. All of a sudden the moths I felt in Mr. Peters's class started to fly up inside my belly.

"We're going to check in on Judy Miller. She's student teaching in one of the fourth-grade classes," he said. Then Cora handed me a pad and a pen for taking notes.

When we got to the fourth-grade class, Judy Miller welcomed us inside. She said, "Class, we have some special visitors. This is Frankly Miller. She is Principal for the Day."

It gave me a **good day feeling** that she told everyone about calling me Frankly. I took out my notepad and wrote down *Judy Miller is friendly.*

"Hi, Frankly!" everyone called at once because they were so **excitified** to get to meet the actual winner of the Principal for the Day contest.

"Hi, every single person!" I said.

"Frannie's job today is to watch student teachers in action and report on the good things they are doing. So please, don't mind us. We will just be sitting here for a couple of minutes while you work. Thank you," Principal Wilkins said. We sat down on cold, gray stools.

"Thank you, Frankly and Principal Wilkins," Judy said.

I wrote down *Judy Miller is very polite.*

The student teacher had a **professional** piece of paper in her hand. That was the third good thing I wrote down about her.

Judy Miller is very businessish.

When I was finished, I looked at Principal Wilkins and nodded to let him know that I wrote down three things like I was supposed to. Just as we were allowed to barge in without getting yelled at, we got up and walked out without having to say good-bye!

CHAPTER

Cora met me outside of Judy Miller's classroom and reminded me of the next very important part of the day: LUNCH. At lunch, I was supposed to sit with Judy Miller to discuss some of the things I noticed about her work. Cora also told me to meet her after lunch outside the teachers' lounge at exactly one o'clock. That gave me one hour to the exact minute to eat.

Before I looked for Judy Miller, I found Elliott. I wanted to just very quickly tell him about my day and the firing box that I found.

As soon as I reached Elliott, my classmates turned around and started throwing **a million and sixty hundredteen** questions at me through the air. A for instance of what I mean is that I heard these questions: *They let principals eat lunch? Did you make any laws? Are you ever coming back to our class again? Do you get to write our report cards?* A lot of stuff like that.

"How is it?" Elliott asked me. His eyes were so **hugeish**, I was afraid they were going to fall right off of his face.

"It's really fantastical," I said. "And, actually, I'm working right this very second!"

"You don't look very busy,"
Millicent, who was standing behind
Elizabeth in line, said.

"Well, I am," I told her. "I just
finished a machillion jobs and have
half a chillion left. In fact, I am not
even supposed to be talking to you.
I am supposed to be sitting with that
student teacher," I said, pointing to
where Judy Miller had just set down
her tray.

"I wish you could eat with us,"
Elliott said. This gave me a bad day
feeling on my skin because I really
wanted to eat with him, too.

I looked back over at the student
teacher table, and since Judy Miller
had not even taken one tiny bite of
her lunch, I knew I could wait just one
more little minute. That is when I got

a very good idea. A very good idea that would be **extremely fast**, as a matter of fact.

"Are you really extra hungry?" I asked Elliott.

He looked down at his stomach, which I guess told him that he wasn't so hungry because when he looked back up

at me, he said, "I don't think so."

"Good. I want to quickly show you my office!"

"I've seen the principal's office already," he said.

"Elliott!" I scolded.

"What?" he asked, a little bit **confusified**.

"You have never seen it when I was principal. Only when Mr. Wilkins was principal," I said, a little bit strictish.

That's when I saw his face channel change, which meant he knew there was a very big difference.

"Sorry, Frannie," he apologized.

"Frankly!" I corrected.

"Frankly!" he said. "Let's go!"

"Where are you going?" Elizabeth asked, **nosy-ish**. "You aren't allowed to leave the cafeteria without an adult."

"I am an adult," I told her.

"No, you're not! You're just a pretend one."

"No, I am actually a real one today. And, if you must know, I was going to show Elliott my office."

"Can I come, too?" Elizabeth asked.

"And me?" Millicent lowered her book and asked.

It was a little **nervousing** that all these people wanted to come with me and see how professional I was. I didn't want them to get in trouble, but how could I say no?

CHAPTER

10

"Let's go quickly then," I said, turning to rush out of the cafeteria when the lunch monitor wasn't looking.

The three of them followed me all the way up the stairs and down all the hallways to my very **fancy** office.

Since it was *my* office, I got to walk in first. I showed them what it looked like when I sat at the desk. Once I was at the desk, I realized that they had never seen me on the phone in the principal's office. I picked up the phone and pretended someone was on the other end. But they didn't look so **impresstified**. So I put my briefcase up on the desk and took out my dad's empty glasses frames and put those on. Now I was sitting at Principal Wilkins's desk, on the phone, wearing my dad's glasses. That was going to really wow them. But, when their faces did not look as **wowish** as they should have, I put my feet up on the desk and leaned back, still holding the phone and wearing glasses so they could see what *that* looked like.

"Frannie, this is boring. Show us something good," Elizabeth said.

"Frankly," I reminded her, "is my professional name."

"Sorry," she said.

"That's okay," I told her.

"Sometimes I forget, too," I admitted.

I let everyone sit in the **swivel chair** for exactly thirty seconds. Then Millicent said that it was time to go

because they'd been there a long time. But I didn't want them to leave. I liked having company in my office.

"Wait, you can't go," I said. "I have to show you something really important."

"What?" Elizabeth asked.

"Yeah, what is it?" Elliott wanted to know also. I hadn't planned on showing this to everyone, but they were all here. So I thought to myself, *Why not?*

I walked over to the other side of the room and stood next to the **beautiful red box**. I pointed to the handle that said PULL FOR FIRE.

"Wow," Elizabeth said.

"What *is* it?" Elliott wanted to know.

"What it is, exactly, is the handle you pull when you are going to fire someone."

"Really? That's how you fire someone?" Elliott asked me.

"Yes, it is a scientific fact that you fire someone by pulling that big, red handle."

"What does it do, though? When you

pull the handle?" Elliott wanted to know. Elliott and I had very similar brains. That is why he and I thought a lot of the same things.

"I don't know exactly," I admitted.

"We should probably go," Elizabeth said, looking at the clock. I could not believe it! This was the most interesting thing she was ever going to see in her **worldwide** life, and she wanted to *go*? I did not want them to leave. I wanted them to see more about my job and be a little more impresstified with all my office business. I had to do something to keep them there. Just for a few minutes longer. And that is why I put my hand on the beautiful red handle.

"Let's see what happens when you pull it," I said. I expected Millicent to say no because she is very rule-ish, but she didn't. No one said anything. The three of them looked at me with their impresstified eyeballs. That is when my hand felt **a little nervous** about what my mouth had just said.

CHAPTER 11

I was holding the handle so hard, I thought I could feel the red of it on my hand. I wondered if holding the handle was **against the law**.

"Are you really going to pull it?" Elliott asked me, like he really wanted me to say yes.

I had a bad day feeling on my skin. And that bad day feeling on my skin said, "Are you absolutely positive you should be doing this?"

Millicent looked at the clock, and I had to get her attention. That is why I ignored the bad day feeling and pulled the handle all the way down.

You will not even believe your ears about what happened: An **actual alarm** went off! When you fire someone, everyone in the entire world must know because that is how loud exactly the alarm sounded.

Everyone was so shocktified that we couldn't move for an entire year. Millicent put both hands over her ears and then so did Elizabeth. That's when I got the geniusal idea to push the handle back up so the **horrendimous** noise would go away. But when I pushed the handle back up, the horrendimous noise continued! There was no stopping it at all.

A few seconds later, we heard Principal Wilkins yelling for Cora. And then, a few seconds after that, Principal Wilkins's shadow was at our feet, and when we looked up, he was standing over us. His face was as big and red as the firebox, and his mouth hung open in a *you kids are in a year of trouble!* expression.

Two centimeters of a second later, Cora appeared behind him wearing the exact same face as Principal Wilkins. We did not know what to do. Except for Elizabeth. She knew what to do, and what she did exactly was point a finger at me to say "She did it!"

Instead of yelling at us, Principal Wilkins ran to his desk, opened his secret drawer, pulled out the microphone, and started to shout into it.

"Please stay where you are. This is a false alarm. There is no fire, and this is not a fire drill. Please stay where you are!" Principal Wilkins shuffled us out of the office and into the hall. We followed him down to the lunch room where **fifteen million kids** were

wondering what was happening. Some looked scared and confused. Principal Wilkins waved his arms in the air. He was yelling, but it was hard to hear him over the loud, screaming alarms. He was trying to tell everyone to stay where they were.

Some kids heard, but some didn't, and that is why they were acting **jumpy and worried**. I looked over at all the crammed kids and saw a girl crying. Her friend had an arm around her, and when she saw me looking, she explained, "She's really scared of fire."

"There isn't really a fire," I told the crying girl. "This is just a big mistake." But she didn't seem to believe me because she cried even harder.

Suddenly a lot of kids ran to the windows. When I looked outside, my head almost fell off my body. **Three fire trucks** were pulling up right in front of our school!

CHAPTER 12

A **millionteen and seven** firemen wearing black and yellow bumblebee uniforms got off the truck and raced inside the building. Principal Wilkins ran after them, trying to explain that this was a false alarm, but they said they still needed to check out the building.

I turned around and saw Elliott, Millicent, and Elizabeth. They were all looking very worried, but not in a "there might be a fire" kind of way. It was a "I

hope I'm not going to get in trouble"
type of way! That's when I realized I
wasn't going to be the only one who got
in trouble.

But I wouldn't let that happen.
I would just explain everything to
everyone and any **confusified** feelings
would just go away.

Suddenly, my ears felt like they were filling up. Something was different. There were big sighs of relief all around me, and that's when my ears realized that they weren't full at all, but empty. The alarm had stopped, and the firemen were leaving the school. A lot of the kids waved to them,

and they waved back. Even though I
love waving at firemen, I didn't because
of the **bad day feeling**.

"Can I have everyone's attention?"
Principal Wilkins called. "I know
that was frightening for some people,
but everything is okay now. That was
a false alarm. I don't want anyone to
worry. Now, we have only six minutes
left of lunch, so please hurry and finish
your food. We've lost some time, but
that does not mean you can be late for
your classes."

"Six minutes?!" someone called out
with a lot of complaining in his voice.

"That's not enough time!" someone
else called.

"No, it certainly isn't, but we must
face the facts, and those are our facts.
Now, hurry up and get back to your

tables," Principal Wilkins said.

My line started to hurry up and move, and I jogged to keep up because they were going really fast. Just as I was about to pass Principal Wilkins, he said, "Not so fast, young lady." Then he signaled for Elliott, Elizabeth, and Millicent to come over. Once they reached us, Principal Wilkins said, "You know you are not supposed to leave the cafeteria without adult supervision."

"But, Frannie—" Elizabeth interrupted, but Principal Wilkins put his hand up to stop her.

"You are your own responsibility, and Frannie is her own responsibility. I want the three of you to write me a composition on why you think I have this rule in the first place."

The three of them okayed Principal Wilkins, and he told them they could get back in line, but I could not. I followed behind him as we went back to my office, which was really his office. When he sat in the chair that I'd been sitting in all day, a **big disappointment puddle** dripped at my feet.

"Have a seat, Frances," he said. *Uh-oh. Principal Wilkins Frances-ed me. That is never a good sign.*

Principal Wilkins looked at me with a very sad day kind of face.

"Am I in trouble?" I asked.

"Yes, Frances. You're in quite a bit of trouble," he said. That sentence did not make me feel very fantastical. "It's quite serious what you did. What if there had been an actual fire somewhere else?"

This was **confusifying**. "What do you mean?"

"All the firemen in Chester were here with all their equipment, but there was no fire to put out. What if, across town, there had been a fire—a real one? Who would have been there to put that fire out? Do you understand what I'm saying?"

I did **indeed and nevertheless** see what he was saying. But when he said this, I understood just how seriousal of a crime it was I committed.

"I'm glad that no one got hurt," I said.

"Me too. You were very lucky that no one got hurt. I'm afraid this is your third strike, Frannie." I hung my head.

"What is going to happen to me

now?" I asked. I really did not want to go to jail.

"Since you were Principal for the Day, and it's the principal's job to discipline the students, I'd like you to come up with your own punishment."

My **eyeballs** almost popped off my entire face, and I took off my glasses.

"Punish myself?" I could not even believe my ears about this news.

"Yes, Frances. Please go join your class, and when you have come up with a suitable punishment, come back and tell me what it is," he said.

"Okay," I said. I walked out of his office with my face hanging down to my **shoelaces**. I passed Cora but was too humilified to say good-bye. I had been **fired** from the best job I barely even had.

CHAPTER 13

I did not like all the looks my
classmates gave me when I slunked
back into Mrs. Pellington's class.
They murmured and even mouthed
things to me, but I pretended not to
notice. I sat near Elliott, and he stared
at me so hard I knew he was trying
to get inside my brain. I was too
embarrassed to look at him. Instead,
I wrote something down on a piece
of paper and passed it to Elliott. The

paper said, "I was fired!"

In a halfteen second I got a note back from Elliott. It read, "That is too bad. I am a little bit mad at you."

When I read those words, my stomach **almost burst** into tears. I did not like when anyone was mad at me, but especially Elliott. I looked at him with the saddest eyes of the world, but he didn't look back.

As we were walked to art class, I went over to Millicent, Elizabeth, and Elliott.

"I'm very sorry that I ruined your entire lives," I told them. "If it makes you feel better, I got fired."

Elizabeth and Millicent gasped, but Elliott didn't because he already knew about that part.

"I forgive you, Frankly," Elliott

said, even though I could tell he wasn't all the way back to happy.

"Me too," Millicent said. I looked at Elizabeth.

"I'll think about it," she said.

I told them that I had to punish my own self. That is the part Elizabeth seemed to like best. She sat right next to me in art class and said she would help me with some ideas.

"How about if you have to apologize to me, Millicent, and Elliott again?" was Elizabeth's very **terrible** idea.

"But I already did that," I said.

"Well, I didn't accept!" she said.

"I am very, very sorry, Elizabeth," I said. "I really did not mean to get you into trouble."

Elizabeth scrunched up her mouth in a way that said she did not like that

I did exactly what she wanted. She is very **confusifying** in this way.

"Okay . . . ," Elizabeth said with a big sigh. "You are forgiven. Sort of."

"What if . . . ," Millicent started before staring into space.

"What if, what?" Elliott asked her.

"What if"—Millicent turned back to us—"you had to work at the fire department?"

I loved that idea, but my parents would never, ever let me. "I'm not even allowed to turn on the stove by myself," I told her.

"Me neither," said Millicent.

"How about you have to clean Principal Wilkins's house for a month?" Elliott asked, but I scrunched my face at that idea.

"Or mow his lawn for twenty-four

years?" Elizabeth threw in.

I did not prefer any of these suggestions **whatsoever**.

That is when I came up with my own idea.

"What if . . . ," I started as they leaned in to hear what geniusal idea I was going to have. "I agreed not to work again for anyone else, for at least one entire week?"

"That's a really good idea!" Elliott said, nodding. "That would be really hard for you since you're very jobbish."

"And punishments are supposed to be hard," I added.

That's when I asked our art teacher for a hall pass. I had to speak to Principal Wilkins about very important and very **principalish** business!

CHAPTER

I was so excitified to tell Principal Wilkins my punishment, but Cora made me wait for **a year and a hundred**. Finally, she let me talk to Principal Wilkins. I sat down in the chair where the bad students sit and looked at him right in the eyeballs.

"Principal Wilkins," I began. "For my punishment, I will not take another job, anywhere in the world, not even president of the United

States, for one entire week. That is seven whole days."

"Frannie, that is not a punishment," he told me.

"Yes, it is, Principal Wilkins, because I am a really jobbish person, and a punishment is when you make someone do something that is hard for them. Not working is really hard for me."

"Do you have any job offers?" he asked.

"No," I told him.

"Don't you need to have something before it can be taken away?" he asked me.

That question **stumpified** me.

"A punishment is hard because you have to make a sacrifice. A sacrifice is when you give something up that you don't want to give up. Like an event."

I looked at him very hard because I wanted to read his **brain notes** to see what he was talking about. But they were too far in his head for me to read.

"Think about things that you were looking forward to doing and don't want to give up. Perhaps giving up one of those things would be a good punishment. Do you have anything coming up that you were looking forward to?"

I shook my head no.

"Well, why don't you think about it and come back when you find something."

"Okay," I told him and slunked toward the door. I could barely believe my own ears that he didn't love my idea. Just as I was walking out the door, I thought of something.

"My presentation," I said.

"Frances," he said. "You had three strikes. You are no longer allowed to give a presentation."

"Maybe instead of a presentation, I can apologize to everyone?" I asked.

"That sounds good to me," he said.

"And I could also come in on Saturday and help clean up the school," I offered.

"Frannie, I think we've found ourselves the perfect punishment."

CHAPTER 15

Principal Wilkins gave me twenty minutes to write my speech. When the bell rang for the afternoon assembly, I followed him to the auditorium with a very bad day feeling on my skin. From behind the curtain I saw all the kids file in and take their seats. My entire insides were filled up with **moths and butterflies**. Then things got quiet and my hands got sweaty and my mouth got dry. I did not even hear what Principal Wilkins said into the silver ball of the microphone. I just saw him wave me out onto the stage.

Not even one person clapped for me.

I stood up on a **special box** so I would be taller and put my mouth near the microphone.

"Hello to everyone," I said.

"Hello," they mumbled back.

"I did not do a very good job as Principal for the Day. A for instance of what I mean is that I got fired." Everyone made shocktified noises. "I got fired because I pulled a handle that was actually the fire alarm."

I looked over at Elliott, who still looked a little **upsettish** with me.

"I was trying to show off, which is why I got into trouble. I did not think about what I was doing. If I had, I would not have pulled the handle. I know now that what I did was very dangerous because I used up all the firemen in town for a fire that wasn't a fire. I am very sorry. I hope that you will forgive me. Thank you very much for listening to every single word that came out of my mouth. I hope you will not fire me from your lives."

I got off the stage and joined my class. Elliott looked at me and gave a little bit of a smile, but he did not give me a thumbs-up. The bad day feeling on my skin did not go away.

Principal Wilkins had called my parents and told them what happened. That is a for instance of why my mom picked me up from school, and I didn't go home with Elliott like usual. She had her **scoldish** face on when I got into the car. That is why I told her that very first second that I already did my punishment and that I came up with it all by myself.

"I heard," she told me. "I bet that was very hard for you."

"I was humilifed when no one clapped for me," I told her. "I'm glad it's over. And I have to go to school on Saturday."

This was something she didn't know about.

"I said I'd help clean up the entire school on Saturday."

My mom leaned over and patted my leg. "Good job, Frances. I'm proud of you for that."

We drove away from school toward home. Nearly halfway there, we saw the fire station, and just as we were about to pass it, I got a **geniusal** idea.

"Pull over, Mom!" I called. She smiled without looking at me, like she knew exactly what I was going to do. She pulled over near the **fire station**, and we got out. The big, red garage door was rolled all the way up, so there wasn't a door or anything for me to knock on. We just walked straight in. All the firemen were there, and they turned and smiled at us.

"The tour doesn't start until five PM," one called out.

"I'm not here for a tour," I said.

"Oh? Then how can we help you?" the man wanted to know.

"I was the one who set off the fire alarm at Chester Elementary School today," I confessed.

"Why would you do that?" a

youngish man asked.

I looked down at the ground. "I thought it was what you pulled when you fired someone. I was showing off because I was Principal for the Day," I explained.

A couple of them laughed.

"I just wanted to say that I'm sorry I ruined your lives and made you come out there when there wasn't a fire."

"Can I tell you a secret?" one of them asked.

I loved secrets, so I nodded very hard.

"It happens a lot."

"It does?" I asked, my eyes so big they almost flew out of my head. "But it's very dangerous."

"It is very dangerous," one of them agreed. "I'm very glad you know that. Maybe you can help us spread the word."

I loved the idea of helping the firemen by spreading the word.

"How about we give you a tour, anyway?" one of the firemen asked.

"I'm in the middle of a punishment," I explained. "Can I come another time?"

"Sure," they said.

I looked at my mom and then back at the firemen.

"That might not be for a lot of years," I said. "But I'll see what I can do."

THE END.

Want more Frannie?

Check Out All the Books in the Series Including

Frankly, Frannie: Fashion Frenzy
Coming Soon!

Frannie is in a mother-daughter fashion show!
Mrs. Miller can't wait—but Frannie feels that
being a designer for the show would be much
more workerish than modeling. Can Frannie
find a way to shine?

Visit **FranklyFrannie.com**

- Make your own business cards and résumé
- Write a very official letter
- Make your own sock doll
- Take a quiz to find out your perfect job
- Read all about Frannie's books
  ...and more!